The Call of the Wild

by
Jack London

adapted by
Mitsu Yamamoto

Illustrations by
Pablo Marcos Studio

MOBY BOOKS

Published by Playmore Inc., Publishers,
230 Fifth Avenue, New York, N.Y. 10001
and Waldman Publishing Corp.,
570 Seventh Avenue, New York, N.Y. 10018

ILLUSTRATED CLASSIC EDITIONS

edited by

Malvina G. Vogel

Copyright © 1979 by
Playmore Inc., Publishers and Waldman Publishing Corp.,
New York, New York

MOBY BOOKS is a registered trademark
of Waldman Publishing Corp., New York, New York

Printed in Canada

Contents

About the Author

Jack London was born in San Francisco, California, on January 12, 1876. Even though he quit school at 14, London was a great reader. While still in his teens, he worked as a coal-shoveler, a jute mill worker, and an oyster pirate in America, and then as a seal hunter in Japan and Siberia.

Returning home from this expedition, London became a tramp and was jailed for vagrancy.

In 1897, after the Gold Rush started, 21-year-old London went prospecting in Canada and Alaska. There, he learned about the lives of trappers, Indians, gold prospectors—and very importantly—sled-dogs. His experiences in the North formed the basis for many of his adventure books, especially his best-sellers, *The Call of the Wild, White Fang,* and *The Sea Wolf.*

During his 17-year writing career, London wrote 50 books, novels, and short stories in addition to newspaper articles and political essays.

By the time he was 40, London had earned a million dollars through his writing, but his own personal suffering led him to leave man's world, just as it led Buck, his *Call of the Wild* dog hero. And on November 22, 1916, Jack London committed suicide. He had experienced more of life than most people, and he told the world about it in a fascinating, vigorous, and memorable style.

Dogs You Will Read About

Buck, *a St. Bernard-Scotch shepherd who is kidnapped and taken to the North*

Spitz, *a large snow-white sled-dog and Buck's enemy*

Curly, *a friendly Newfoundland and Buck's friend*

Billee
Sol-leks
Dave
Joe } *other sled-dogs who are part of Buck's team*
Pike
Dub
Dolly

Skeet
Nig } *John Thorton's pets*

People You Will Read About

Judge Miller, *Buck's original owner*

Manuel, *the gardener who kidnaps Buck*

François }
Perrault } *Canadian officials who train Buck to be a sled-dog*

Morgan, *a dealer in stolen dogs*

Charles }
Hal }
Mercedes } *three clumsy prospectors who buy Buck*

John Thornton, *a gold prospector who befriends Buck*

Hans }
Pete } *Thorton's partners*

"Black" Burton, *an evil, malicious prospector*

The Yeehats, *an Indian tribe of the North*

"Morning, Buck. How's My Big Dog?"

CHAPTER 1

Buck Is Betrayed

The day that changed Buck's life began like every other day on Judge Miller's California estate. The Judge called to him for an early morning walk, patting him briskly.

"Morning, Buck. How's my big dog?" the Judge asked. For an answer, Buck tossed his large head, with its long, healthy gray fur. His size—one hundred forty pounds—came from his father, a St. Bernard. But it was his mother, a Scotch shepherd dog, who had given the long, wolf-like shape to his nose and jaws.

Buck and the Judge visited the stables and the kennels, where smaller dogs eyed Buck enviously. The Judge's two sons, wet from a swim in the pool, invited Buck into the water, but Buck preferred a dignified walk with his best friend, the Judge. Their final stop was in the garden to see how the late autumn flowers were doing. Here, Manuel, the gardener's helper, smiled to himself when he saw Buck. Only Manuel knew that this proud pet was having his last walk in the warm sun on Judge Miller's estate.

After dinner, Buck lay at the Judge's feet in front of the fireplace and watched the flames. The old man talked to him like another person, saying, "Buck, men are mad with gold fever. They're deserting their families and running away North to the Klondike. They're not prepared for the bitter cold up there or the hardships of a half-civilized country. But even now, in 1897, some men

Manuel Has an Evil Plan.

will do anything for money."

And that same night, Manuel, beset by heavy gambling debts, proved how right the Judge was.

After the Judge went to bed, Manuel called softly to Buck. Buck knew Manuel to be a friend and went to him. With a quick movement, Manuel doubled a rope around Buck's neck. Buck wore an expensive collar with his name and the Judge's name on it. But he had never felt a coarse rope like this one around his neck before. He looked up at Manuel questioningly, but the man would not meet his gaze. Manuel gave the rope a tug and hurried out to the road that led past the gate of the estate. Buck obeyed the pull on the rope and trotted beside him.

There, a car was waiting with its engine running. Manuel did not speak to the driver. He simply opened the back door and tugged Buck into the back seat with him. Buck

Buck Answers a Friendly Voice.

climbed in willingly. He loved a ride, but this one was over in a few moments. When Manuel hurried him out of the car, Buck recognized the local train station. A burly man, almost twice the size of Manuel, was waiting in the shadows.

"You timed it pretty close," he complained. "Train's due about now."

"I had to wait for the old man to go to bed," said Manuel. "Where's my money?"

The big man was ready and immediately handed Manuel some money. Then he reached for the rope that held Buck. Buck growled softly, but the man did not retreat at the warning. He quickly seized the rope ends from Manuel and gave them a slight twist. In the middle of another growl, Buck found his breath cut off. Now angry, he tried to spring at the stranger. The man met him halfway, grabbed him by the collar, and easily flipped him onto his back. Then the man tightened

Stolen and Sold!

the rope. Buck struggled, but felt his strength ebbing when he could not breathe. His eyes glazed, and his chest heaved in a desperate need for air. Then Buck slumped down on the station platform, unconscious. He did not hear the train stop or feel himself being lifted aboard.

Now a nightmare began for Buck. The big man rode beside him in the baggage car. At Buck's first move toward him, he tightened the rope and Buck again knew nothing. In a daze he felt himself being lifted off the train and pushed roughly into a cage. The cage was loaded onto another train and for two days and nights, Buck rode. No one fed him or gave him water. Soon he was sick from an inflammation of his parched throat.

Buck had always been pampered by the Judge, so he was shocked by the cruel treatment he was receiving from the big man. He was not quite unconscious from the rope-

A Train Trip to—Where?

twisting when he felt the man untying the rope. Buck gathered all his weak forces and bit down quickly on the cruel hand. The man drew back with a curse and gave Buck a kick in the ribs. A welcome blackness came to Buck along with the pain.

Morning! Activity! Bustling in the baggage car! Buck's cage was thrown carelessly into a car and delivered to the back room of a saloon. Buck lifted his sick head and looked around in amazement. The room was crammed with dogs in cages. All the dogs were large, but Buck was the largest. And in the middle of the room sat Morgan, the man in charge. He was not very tall, but he had wide, strong shoulders, and—most important of all—he had a club.

This club in Morgan's big fist began Buck's education for the new world he was entering.

A Bite and a Kick!

Hatred for the Man with the Club

CHAPTER 2

The Rule of the Club

The four men who had carried in Buck's cage let it down with a bang. One of them wiped a dirty hand across his forehead.

"Here's a red-eyed monster for you, Morgan," he said to the man with the club.

Morgan got up from his chair and slowly walked over to Buck's cage. Buck stood up, baring his teeth. The two opponents faced each other for the first time. Instant hatred flamed through Buck, strengthening his weakened body. He hurled himself at the unyielding bars of his cage.

"Open it up!" ordered Morgan, smiling a grim smile that held no amusement.

"He's awful mad," answered one man. "Maybe you ought to let him calm down some."

As an answer, Morgan seized a hatchet and chopped off the padlock on Buck's cage with one heavy, well-placed blow.

"Get out of the way!" shouted a man. They scattered to the corners of the room, one man even perching himself on a dog's cage.

Buck threw himself against the cage door. It flew open. His leap broken for a second, he regathered his powers and launched himself at Morgan like a rocket.

While he was in mid-air, snarling with his jaws open, Buck received a shock on his back that felt as if he had been struck by lightning. He fell to the ground. He had never been hit by a club before and did not understand what had happened. But in a second he was

Morgan Chops Off the Padlock.

up and flying at Morgan once more. Again the terrible shock came as Morgan slammed the club across Buck's shoulders. Buck went down again. This time he was aware that it was the club in Morgan's fist that was bringing him down. But there was no way to avoid it. Buck kept springing for Morgan's throat, but each time, the club cut him down with a pain that jarred his whole body. Buck never reached Morgan.

After a dozen blows, Buck could no longer stand up, much less spring at the man. Then Morgan advanced and, taking careful aim, hit Buck on the nose with full force. All the pain that Buck had endured was nothing compared to the agony of this last blow. It crumpled him completely. And the room, Morgan, the other man, and the dogs faded from his sight into blackness.

When Buck's senses returned, he still lay where he had fallen. His collar was now in

The Terrible Shock of the Club!

Morgan's hand along with the club, and the man was reading his name.

Then Morgan spoke in a voice that held no anger. "Now, Buck, you know who is master here. Behave, and there'll be no clubbing."

He reached out his left hand and patted Buck on his bleeding head. Buck did not have the strength to bite that hand even if he wanted to. Yet, though he hated Morgan, he did not want to bite him. Buck understood that he was now under the Rule of the Club. The club had beaten him, but it had not broken him. It was a lesson to be learned, Buck reasoned. In this new life, a dog stood no chance against a man with a club. So Buck gladly accepted the water and food that Morgan brought him. And in the next few weeks, he made no move toward Morgan. He simply ate, drank, and recovered his strength as his wounds healed.

Buck Has Learned the Rule of the Club.

Dogs Are Sold.

CHAPTER 3

Buck Is Sold

While Buck was recovering from his wounds, he saw large, furry dogs in cages arrive daily. Others also left daily after visits from rough-spoken men who looked at all of Morgan's dogs, pointed at a few of them, and handed Morgan money. Helpers carried the cages from the room, and Buck never saw the dogs in them again. These acts frightened Buck, and each time he was glad that the strangers did not point at him.

But the day came when Buck's strength returned, and he looked once again like the healthy dog that Judge Miller had owned. Morgan was showing a small man around the room. The man spoke English with a French accent and moved quickly from cage to cage. He needed only a glance to decide "yes" or "no" about a dog.

He stopped in front of Curly's cage. Curly was a good-natured Newfoundland who had arrived soon after Buck. She had easily settled down to Morgan's routine of food, no exercise, and no trouble. Now the stranger looked at Curly's teeth and her feet. He felt her legs and chest. Curly bore the examination patiently, her eyes trusting.

"She good dog. I take her," said the man. He quickly passed the next four cages and stopped in front of Buck's. There, he drew in a deep breath as if in surprise. His eyes lit up, and he smiled.

"Hey, now, Morgan," said the stranger, "here is wonderful dog. Heavy dog with

A Stranger Buys Curly.

strong muscles for work. Good furry coat protect him from frost. Where you find dog like this?"

Morgan scowled. "No questions here. If you want the dog, just pay your money."

The man knelt down and opened Buck's cage. With a gentle hand he felt Buck's legs and chest and opened his mouth. Finally he examined each of Buck's feet. Buck stood quietly, knowing that Morgan and his club were close by. But he trembled because he felt that soon he would be leaving with this stranger. Though he hated Morgan, at least Morgan and the roomful of dogs were something that he was used to.

Though Buck had not suffered any illtreatment after Morgan's awful beating, he had not received any friendliness either. But now this stranger was running a calloused hand over his head and under his chin. The man's touch and his kind eyes reminded

"Where You Find Dog Like This?"

Buck of Judge Miller.

"Ah, you know friend, do you not?" said the man, rubbing in back of Buck's ear.

To the man's question of how much was wanted for Buck, Morgan answered, "Three hundred. The Canadian Government can afford that. This is one dog in a thousand."

The stranger handed Morgan the money and said, "Not one dog in a thousand. He is one dog in *ten* thousand. Let's go."

Buck's cage was latched, and Morgan's helpers carried it out to a waiting wagon. Then Curly's cage was lifted on. The two dogs exchanged a look that combined fear and excitement. Then their eyes followed the little man as he got into the front seat of the wagon.

The two dogs never looked back. That part of their lives was over. They were only concerned about the future.

The Stranger Pays Morgan.

A Last Look at Warm Weather

CHAPTER 4

Snow!

The man who had bought Buck and Curly was named Perrault. He was a French-Canadian and worked for the Canadian Government. He and his partner, François, carried important official messages by dog sled, and speed of delivery was their main concern.

Perrault and François sailed from Seattle, Washington, aboard a ship called the *Narwhal*. Buck stood on deck with Curly and took his last look at warm weather, although he did not know this at the time. Perrault took

37

them below deck to meet two other large dogs. One was Dave—a gloomy, sleepy dog who wanted only to be left to himself. The other greeted Buck and Curly with a superior air, though he smiled. He was a handsome fellow, snow-white, and almost as big as Buck. This was Spitz, a dog accustomed to leading and being admired by men and dogs alike. Curly was awed by Spitz.

But neither Perrault nor François showed much friendliness to the dogs. Even though he had admired and patted Buck earlier, Perrault now maintained a distance. However, he treated all the dogs alike, with fairness. The beautiful Spitz got no larger a dinner than gloomy Dave.

But Spitz was not used to being treated the same as lesser dogs, and he decided to assert himself. Smiling, he approached Buck at dinner. When Buck looked up, Spitz snatched his food. Buck sprang to punish him, but at

Buck Meets Dave and Spitz.

that same moment, Perrault's whip lashed through the air and encircled Spitz. With a howl Spitz dropped Buck's bone. Buck halted his leap, picked up his bone, and went back to enjoying his dinner. Spitz had been punished by the fair Perrault, and Buck felt that was enough. But he saw Spitz staring at him with anger barely concealed in his snapping black eyes.

Though it was only a moment between the stealing of Buck's bone and Buck's taking it back, Curly had started to bark in anxiety and excitement. Dave, however, looked up once and then resumed his own dinner as if nothing were happening. Buck soon saw that nothing could disturb Dave.

When the *Narwhal* started to pitch and roll in a storm, Buck and Curly, never having been on the water before, were half-wild with fear. But Dave only gave them an annoyed glance and went to sleep. This helped to

Perrault Punishes Spitz.

shame Buck into calmness, though Curly continued to yelp and race around in fear.

The *Narwhal* plodded on, farther and farther North. When the two men took the dogs for a run on deck twice a day, Buck felt the change in the weather. It was an icy kind of cold that caused the dogs' fur coats to ruffle up. But that way, the fur held in their body heat better.

One morning when Buck woke up, he immediately sensed that something was different. In a moment he realized that the steady throb of the *Narwhal's* propeller was silent. The ship was no longer making her way against rough seas. She was in port.

Perrault and François rushed around packing their belongings. Finally François brought out the dogs' leashes, and they lined up eagerly. They were infected by the excitement of the men and the knowledge that the *Narwhal* had stopped.

A Run on the Deck

Buck was the first to follow François up onto the deck. But his feet sank down into something white and mushy—something like mud. He jumped back with a snort. Then he noticed that more white stuff was falling through the air and landing on his coat. He shook it off, but more continued to fall. He sniffed at it curiously, then licked some up on his tongue. It bit like fire, and in the next instant it was gone. This puzzled him. He tried it again, with the same result. François and the deck hands laughed uproariously, pointing at Buck and at the white stuff they called "snow." Then, more confident, Buck lifted his huge head and let the snow fall freely onto his face. It made him feel almost playful.

Perrault and François led Buck and the other dogs down the gangplank of the *Narwhal.* The snow was falling steadily, but Buck padded along easily, not frightened, not cold. He had begun to master his new surroundings.

Buck Is Puzzled by the Snow.

A Mining Camp in the Far North

CHAPTER 5

Buck Learns a Job and a Lesson

Buck's ease did not last long. He and the other dogs were immediately taken to a mining camp where they were forced to become part of a noisy and dangerous life. There were hundreds of rough men, very few of them fair like Perrault and François. And all of them had whips and clubs. Their dogs were even worse. Buck had to be alert every moment.

The Husky dogs around him were unlike any town dogs he had known when he lived with Judge Miller. These brutes were constantly looking for a fight. And they gave no warning. Buck had never been a timid dog, but now he walked warily, not wanting to provoke these strong, angry animals.

He and Curly had only a day to get used to their new neighbors before their two owners thrust them into another new experience. François brought out an arrangement of straps and buckles, and fastened it onto Buck. Buck knew it was a harness, for the horses in Judge Miller's stable had worn such things. François then took the next step. He connected the harness by long straps and reins to a sled.

"Now, Buck, mush, mush!" commanded François, seated on the sled and waving his whip in the air. Buck looked back at the man in confusion. He saw that François was making forward motions with his body and pointing ahead while calling, "Mush, mush! Now Buck, mush!"

Buck Is Fitted with a Harness.

Though Buck did not see the point of this activity, he understood that François wanted him to move ahead and pull the sled behind him. Buck did not like being used as a horse, but he knew that François always demanded strict obedience. So Buck set off, guided by a tug on the reins to the left.

Soon they were in a nearby forest. François hopped off the sled and let Buck rest while he chopped firewood. In spite of the added weight of the wood on the sled, Buck still pulled easily, and they were soon back in camp. As he unhitched the sled, François grinned approval at Buck.

The next day François hitched the other dogs to the sled. They were lined up in a row with Spitz in the lead and Dave nearest the sled. Then François buckled the harness around Buck and placed him in front of Dave. The other dogs were eager to start, and at François' call of "Mush!" they leaped ahead.

Buck Pulls the Sled Easily.

The quick start surprised Buck and as he scrambled to keep up, he felt Dave nip his hindquarters as a punishment for not being ready.

François waved his whip over their heads, but he only touched a dog with it if the dog lagged and slowed the entire team, or if the dog made a wrong turn. As the lead-dog, Spitz also helped discipline the team by throwing his weight to one side or the other. The jerk forced the other dogs into the direction he wanted.

Buck pulled hard and concentrated hard on doing it right. When François finally called "Ho!" Buck was glad to stop. The unusual work tired him at first. He also had difficulty in coordinating with the other dogs. But by the end of the second day, he began to enjoy the pulling. It was another challenge, and Buck gained a sense of pride in meeting it and winning.

The Quick Start Surprises Buck.

That night after dinner, he felt a new comradeship with the dangerous and often treacherous Huskies in the camp. Now he was the equal of them because he did the same work. Of course, Spitz and Dave were far more experienced, and Buck knew there was much to learn. But he felt it would only be a matter of time before he was as able and confident in front of a sled as those two. He wondered if Curly also felt this way about the new work. But when he looked for her, he saw that Curly, always friendly, was approaching a Husky about half her size.

Suddenly, without warning, the Husky leaped in the air. There was a metallic clip of teeth and a leap back! Curly was left with her face ripped open from eye to jaw. This was a wolf's way to fight—a quick strike and a leap back. Buck looked on in horror, but he heard Spitz laugh. All the dogs of the camp were roused. They formed a circle around the

A Husky Attacks Curly.

small Husky and the wounded Curly, waiting intently and licking their chops. It was only later that Buck understood why.

Curly bravely rushed her opponent, but he leaped in, struck again, and was out before she touched him. At the Husky's next strike Curly was knocked off her feet. She never regained them. As soon as she went down, the circle of Huskies closed in for a mass attack. In a moment. . .Curly was dead.

Buck had seen the whole incident, but almost could not believe that dogs would act so viciously toward one another. He heard Spitz laugh again. Then he believed what he had seen. He was surrounded by savages. There was no fair play. Once down on the ground, you were finished. Buck swore to himself that what had happened to Curly would never happen to him. In the back of his mind rang the sound of Spitz's cruel laughter. And Buck knew then that he hated Spitz.

A Mass Attack!

Two New Dogs—Billee and Joe

CHAPTER 6

A Dog in a Nest?

Perrault spent the next morning away from camp trying to buy dogs. The loss of Curly could mean a delay in delivering the government messages. But Perrault was so determined to keep on schedule, he returned after lunch with two more dogs.

"A man is bringing another one to me later," he told François, who was examining the newcomers, Billee and Joe.

These two Huskies were brothers, though Buck would not have guessed it. They were very different in manner. Billee was much like Curly—friendly and always looking for approval. But Joe had a mouth that was twisted into a permanent snarl and eyes that glared angrily.

Spitz immediately rushed forward to teach the brothers that he was the lead-dog. He had no trouble beating up Billee. In fact, by whining and wagging his tail, Billee gave up before Spitz even touched him. Even so, Spitz bit him a few times in the flank before turning on Joe.

Joe rose to his feet and faced Spitz. Spitz growled menacingly and circled Joe. But Joe kept whirling around and facing Spitz with blazing eyes and snarling lips. He feared Spitz, but he was ready to make a fight to the death. Spitz sensed this and dropped back. But to save face, he pretended that he had never intended to attack Joe and went after poor Billee again.

The man who had promised another dog to

Spitz Tries to Show He Is Master.

Perrault brought him into camp before dinner. The dog was long and lean, with one eye and a face well-scarred from fighting.

"His name is Sol-leks," the seller told Perrault. "It means 'Angry One.'"

Sol-leks marched into their midst very slowly and deliberately. Spitz, who had risen when he smelled the stranger's approach, immediately sat down again. This Sol-leks was not a dog to tangle with.

But it was Buck's misfortune to tangle with Sol-leks for a first and last time. Though Sol-leks was like Dave in that he wanted only to be left to himself, he had one odd thing about him. He would not permit another dog to approach him on his blind side. Buck, not knowing this, happened to do so on the first night. In a flash, Sol-leks whirled on Buck as he passed and slashed his shoulder down to the bone. Perrault, who had been told about Sol-leks' oddity, interfered

Sol-leks Whirls on Buck.

at once and prevented further trouble. But all the dogs took the warning, and only Buck suffered through ignorance.

With his shoulder paining him and the weather turning even more windy and cold than usual, Buck was uncomfortable and weary. Attracted by the glow of a candle in the tent where Perrault and François slept, Buck slid quietly under the flap into the warmth. But the two men set up a howl of curses at him and bombarded him with cooking pots until he ran back into the snow.

So for an hour Buck wandered about the camp, searching for a warm spot. Savage dogs tried to rush him, but he snarled and saw with satisfaction how they backed down. A heavy snow started falling. Buck was exhausted, and his shoulder throbbed painfully.

Suddenly he had an idea. He would find his teammates and see where they were sleeping.

Buck Is Chased Back into the Snow.

To his astonishment, they had disappeared. With drooping tail and shivering body, he searched for them. Then, near his owners' tent, his fore legs broke through the crust of snow, and he sank down. Something wriggled under his feet. Buck sprang back, bristling and snarling. But a friendly little yelp reassured him. When he investigated the hole, a whiff of warm air greeted him. There, curled up under the snow in a snug ball, lay Billee.

Immediately Buck selected a spot and, with much fuss and wasted effort, managed to dig a hole for himself. He settled in, and soon the heat from his body filled the confined space. At last, in a nest of snow, Buck fell soundly and contentedly asleep.

A Nest in the Snow

Buck Fears a Trap.

CHAPTER 7

On the Trail

The snow continued during the entire night. When the noises of the waking camp roused Buck from sleep, he was completely buried in snow. At first he did not know where he was. Walls of snow pressed on him from every side. A great surge of fear swept through him—the fear of the wild animal for the trap. But Buck was a civilized dog who had known an open cage, but not a trap. Yet some instinct, put there by his fearful ancestors, told him he was in a trap and it was something dangerous. All the muscles in

Buck's body contracted as one. The hair on his shoulders and neck stood straight up. The fear sent him bounding up into the morning light with the snow flying about him in a flashing cloud. Before he had landed on his feet, he remembered about the snow nest.

At Buck's sudden appearance, François called to Perrault with pride, "See Buck! He one intelligent dog. Learn everything."

Perrault had managed to buy three more Huskies. In a short time he and François had harnessed the nine dogs to the sled. Buck was placed between Sol-leks and Dave, who still held the position nearest the sled. Even with his excitement at being harnessed into a full team of dogs, Buck noticed with amazement the change that had come over Sol-leks and Dave. Instead of their usual unconcern and insistence on being alone, they were filled with eagerness and attention to teamwork. They were alert to how the sled rode

Eager for Teamwork

under its load. They could tell in an instant where badly packed snow on the trail might slow the team, and they shifted their weight accordingly. If there was a delay or confusion caused by the other dogs, they grew very irritable.

Buck did his best, but he was still inexperienced. In the first few days he tangled the traces—the straps connecting the harness to the sled—and often did not keep a steady rhythm when he ran. Only then would Dave nip him with sharp teeth, but never otherwise. Or Sol-leks would fly at him for being slow to stand for harnessing. François' whip backed up the two taskmasters in their disciplining.

Soon Buck was rarely nipped, and he began to enjoy the runs. He was infected by the high morale of the team and the two men. Usually Perrault traveled ahead of the dogs, packing the snow with his webbed shoes to

Buck Tangles the Traces.

make it easier for them. He had an expert knowledge of ice and needed only a glance to tell its thickness and possible safety across it for the sled.

The team crossed glaciers and snowdrifts hundreds of feet deep. They went in and out of a dozen camps where gold seekers were waiting for spring to break the ice. On the day that the dogs ran forty miles, Perrault pronounced them the best team he had ever had. Sol-leks turned around to Buck and Dave and gave them a rare smile, which they returned. Buck was filled with a sense of well-being and comradeship. The last thoughts he had that night after nesting down were "forty miles" and "the best team."

Crossing Glaciers and Snowdrifts

No Place for a Slow Eater

CHAPTER 8

The Ancient Song

Buck was always hungry. Running for miles in the icy air and pulling the heavy sled gave him an appetite that could not be satisfied by his ration. He received a pound and a half of sun-dried salmon once a day after the run. Yet the other dogs, because they weighed less and were born to this rough life, received only a pound of the fish. Yet they kept in good condition on it.

For a time Buck received even less than his ration because the other dogs stole any part that he had not yet finished. He had always been a dainty eater and a particular one. So at first the other dogs would finish their fish long before he did and then come after his. There was no way to defend his meal. While he fought off two dogs, the fish would disappear down the throats of the others. There was only one thing to do and Buck did it. He learned to gobble his food as fast as the other dogs did even though his ration was larger.

Constant hunger also forced him to learn another trick, one that would have horrified the Buck who had belonged to Judge Miller. Buck learned to steal and not get caught. After he saw Pike, one of the new dogs, slyly steal a slice of bacon when Perrault's back was turned, he did not need a second lesson. The next day he made off with a whole chunk of bacon. Perrault raised a great fuss about this theft and finally decided that Dub, an awkward, blundering sort of dog, must have

Buck Learns to Steal.

done it. Buck watched Dub get whipped in his place and was not sorry. Rather, he was pleased with his ability to look after himself.

Gradually Buck's muscles became hard as iron. He grew indifferent to all ordinary pain. Also he could eat anything, no matter how disgusting or indigestible. The juices of his stomach then extracted every bit of nutrition from his food, and his body became strong and tough. His sight and scent became remarkably keen, as did his hearing. In his sleep he heard the faintest sound and could decide whether it meant danger or peace. He learned to bite the ice out when it collected between his toes. When he was thirsty and there was a thick layer of ice over the water hole, he would break it by rearing up and striking down with stiff fore legs. One trait of his was not given to the other dogs. Buck could scent the wind and forecast it a night in advance. Even if there was no air when he

Breaking the Ice over the Water Hole

dug his nest for the night, when the wind blew later, he was always in a position where he was sheltered from it.

Not only did Buck learn by experience, but many dead instincts came alive again. Generations of his ancestors who had become domesticated as pets were forgotten. Buck seemed to remember back to the time when wild dogs lived in packs in primitive forests, killing their meat as they ran it down. So it was not difficult for him to learn to fight as his wolf ancestors did, by cutting, slashing, and snapping.

And just as the wolf howled his sad night-time song about life's sorrow, now Buck, too, pointed his nose at the moon and sounded the ancient wolf-like song, loud and clear and mournful.

An Ancient Wolf-Like Song

Spitz Swaggers Before Buck.

CHAPTER 9

The Camp Is Invaded

The hatred between Spitz, the lead-dog, and Buck had continued to grow. Buck knew a fight was sure to come some day, but for the present he preferred to avoid it. He was still busy adjusting to his new life and went out of his way to keep the peace. But Spitz began to imagine that Buck was avoiding their fight because he was timid. So Spitz swaggered before Buck and tried to provoke him, feeling sure that Buck had held his own among all the dogs only because of his huge weight and size. This feeling made Spitz the aggressor on the night they camped on the shore of Lake Le Barge.

Driving snow and a wind that cut like a white-hot knife had forced the men to stop traveling and set up camp early. Buck made a deep nest under a sheltering rock. He was so snug and warm in it that only François distributing the fish rations could have made him leave it. Buck ate quickly and ran back to his nest. But it was occupied—by Spitz!

This act ended Buck's patience. He sprang at Spitz with a roar. Much surprised, Spitz met the charge, and they both tumbled from the nest. They circled one another, snapping, looking for an advantage. Perrault and François, wise in the way of dogs, had known for some time that this fight was due and so now allowed it.

"Give it to him, Buck!" cried François. "He is dirty thief. I, François, say so."

But the fight to the death was not to take

Spitz Steals Buck's Nest.

place that night. Suddenly, there was a loud curse from Perrault as he brought his club down on the bony frame of a wild dog heading for the food box. Then a hoard of forty or fifty wild dogs surged by Perrault. François rushed to rescue the food box, but the wild dogs were maddened by the smell of the food. The box fell to the ground, and its contents scattered. The famished dogs fell on the bread and bacon, and in a few moments not even a crumb remained. The two men beat down a few of the dogs, but there were too many, and they were too fierce to be halted.

The team-dogs, enjoying the fight between Buck and Spitz, at first only looked with astonishment at the invaders. But then the wild dogs turned upon them and attacked viciously. After their first surprise, the team-dogs fought back side by side. Their superior weight and good condition enabled each of them to down two wild dogs at a time. But

Wild Dogs Invade the Camp.

they were outnumbered.

Buck, battling three at a time, saw another dog join in and felt teeth sink into his throat. When he saw it was Spitz, treacherously taking advantage, his rage enabled him to throw off all four dogs.

By now the team-dogs were retreating fighting as they ran into the forest. Buck joined them in flight. The wild dogs did not pursue them, being more interested in finding food at the camp. All the team-dogs had been injured. Dolly, one of the new dogs, had been hurt the worst, with a badly torn throat. They nursed their wounds through the night and limped back into camp at daybreak.

The wild dogs were gone, and Perrault and François were in a very bad mood. Only half the food supply had been saved. The wild dogs had tried to eat everything, even the leather traces and a pair of Perrault' moose-hide moccasins. François examined

The Wild Dogs Tried to Eat Everything.

each dog and shook his head.

"What you think, Perrault? All these bites from mad dogs. Maybe our dogs go mad as well. Why we have such bad luck!"

Perrault shrugged his shoulders. "All we can do is go on. There's four hundred miles between here and Dawson. If it happens, it happens. Let's get under way."

This was easy to say and hard to do. It took the men three hours alone just to repair the chewed traces. The day was half gone before François was ready to shout "Mush!"

Weary and still in pain, the team, nevertheless, picked up their feet together and obeyed. And nobody, not even Buck and Spitz, gave a thought to the unfinished fight between them.

Examining the Wounded Dogs

Perrault Breaks Through the Ice.

CHAPTER 10

Buck Wears Moccasins

The Thirty Mile River was wide open. Its wild, rushing waters did not freeze. Only in the eddies, or quiet places, did the ice take hold at all. Six days of hard work and risk were required to cover those terrible miles on the river's surface.

Perrault, who walked in front of the team, broke through the ice at least a dozen times. Each time, he saved himself with the long pole he carried. He held it up so it fell across the hole made by his body as it went through the ice. François then ran forward and fished

Perrault out. Perrault was almost incapabl
of climbing out by himself because the ic
water at 50° below zero paralyzed him. Tim
was lost from the run while a fire was buil
and Perrault and his clothes were dried.

Once, the sled itself broke through the ice
It dragged Dave and then Buck into the wa
ter. They were half-frozen and all bu
drowned by the time the men rescued them
Their fur were solid coats of ice. Françoi
quickly built a fire, and the men kept th
dogs on the run very close around the fire
sweating and thawing.

Another time, Spitz went through the ic
and dragged the whole team after him up t
Buck. Buck strained backward with all hi
strength. His fore paws were on the slipper
edge of the hole, with the ice all around hin
threatening to crumble. But behind him Dav
strained backward too. And François pulle
back on the sled until his muscles almos

Thawing Out Their Icy Fur

ripped. They were able to hold that way until Perrault fished out the rest of the frozen dripping team.

Apart from the dangerous ice, Buck had another problem. Generations of easy living had softened the feet of his breed of dog. They were not as compact or as hard as the feet of the Huskies. So, all day long Buck limped in agony.

When the run ended, he lay down like a dead dog. Hungry as he was, he would not move to receive his ration of fish, and François had to carry it to him. He also rubbed Buck's feet after dinner each night for a half-hour.

Finally Perrault solved the problem. He sacrificed the tops of his own moccasins to make four moccasins for Buck. This was a great relief. Later Buck found his feet had grown hard to. the trail, and the worn-out shoes were thrown away.

Perrault Makes Moccasins for Buck.

A Proud, Experienced Sled-Dog

CHAPTER 11

Mad Dog!

As the long, hard runs continued day after day, Buck was gripped completely by the pride of the sled-dog. To pull with all one's might, to run fast over the most difficult trail, to work with the men, the sled, and one's fellow dogs like a single machine for covering the miles—this was something to take pride in.

And there were other prides the dogs felt too. Dave, nearest the sled, was known as the wheel-dog. He would have died sooner than give up his special place. And Spitz, as the lead-dog, was in the position of king. It was his privilege to punish the dogs who blundered in the traces or who hid away at harness time in the morning. It was also his glory to stand at the head of the dogs and lead them on the trail.

Buck, far back in the string of dogs, watched enviously every morning as Spitz was harnessed into the lead position. Ambition stirred in Buck, telling him that *he* belonged there. He knew that Spitz must die before he could take his place at the head of the string. Buck waited with great patience for his day of leadership to come.

Though he was master of the team, Spitz was uneasy about Buck. This was the first dog from the South that had proven himself worthy on the trail and in camp. The others had been too soft, dying under the work, the frost, and the starvation. Buck had not only endured, he had prospered and was now the

Buck Envies Spitz, the Lead-Dog.

equal or better of any Husky in strength, savagery, and cunning. Buck worried Spitz.

As François was harnessing up one morning, a long, heartbreaking wolf howl was sounded by Dolly. Its tone made all the dogs bristle with fear. Dolly gave just the one howl, then sprang straight at Buck. Buck saw the mad light in her eye and did not stay to fight, though he could have beaten Dolly easily any other time. Instinct told him this was madness and to run from it.

Buck ran, faster and faster. But Dolly, given added strength from her madness, gained on him. Panting and frothing, she was only a leap behind Buck when he heard François call. Buck doubled back to camp, gasping painfully for air. He was putting all his faith in François to save him. He saw François poised with an upraised axe in his hands. Buck shot by him. Dolly followed, and François brought down the axe. Mad Dolly

Dolly Goes Mad.

was dead, the victim of a bite from one of the mad wild dogs who had invaded the camp a few weeks ago.

Buck staggered over against the sled, exhausted, helpless, and sobbing for breath. Spitz seized this opportunity to spring upon Buck, and his teeth tore the unresisting Buck's flesh to the bone. Suddenly François' lash descended. Buck had the satisfaction of watching Spitz receive the worst whipping ever given to any of the team. This incident decided Buck—he had been on the defensive too long. Now it would be Spitz's turn to defend himself against Buck's actions.

Spitz Attacks the Helpless Buck.

Pike Ignores François' Call.

CHAPTER 12

A Team Divided

Buck became the leader—not of the team, but of a mutiny. One morning after a heavy snowfall, Pike, a lazy dog, would not appear to be harnessed. François called and called. Spitz, furious at Pike's disobedience, raged through the camp, digging in every likely spot. But Pike was well-hidden under a foot of snow.

When Pike was finally found, Spitz jumped to punish him. But Buck flew with equal rage between the two. Spitz was knocked off his feet in surprise. Pike, seeing this, jumped on

Spitz too, and he and Buck tumbled the leader about. François, though he chuckled at the incident, nevertheless had to keep order. He whipped Buck thoroughly, and Spitz whipped Pike equally thoroughly.

In the following days, Buck continued to interfere between Spitz and the dogs that he rightly wanted to punish. But he was careful to do so out of sight of François and his whip. Now general disobedience took over, except for Dave and Sol-leks. There was constant bickering and laziness. Pike even dared to rob Spitz of half a fish, which he then ate under the protection of Buck. Dub and Joe stood up together against Spitz, and he was unable to punish them as they deserved. The dogs lost all awe and fear of Spitz. And Buck never came near him without snarling and bristling.

If the rebellion had been confined to camp, it would not have mattered so much. But it

Pike Dares to Steal Spitz's Fish.

carried over onto the trail. No longer did the team travel as one dog. Now the traces were frequently tangled. Time was lost while two dogs fought or refused to be harnessed. François used his whip constantly, trying to keep peace and to force the dogs to obey the leadership of Spitz as before. He knew Buck was the main troublemaker, but he was never able to catch him in the wrong after the first time when Pike had refused to come out of his nest.

The team pulled into Dawson completely demoralized. Perrault was very late with his messages, which made him quarrel with François for not keeping the dogs in line. And Buck smiled at the ruined reign of Spitz.

Time Is Lost.

Chasing a Snowshoe Rabbit

CHAPTER 13

A Fight to the Death

One night after dinner, Dub turned up a snowshoe rabbit. He dove at it and missed. In a second the whole team was flying after it. They were joined in the chase by fifty Huskies from a Northwest Police camp nearby.

The rabbit sped down the river, then turned off into a small creek. It ran lightly on the surface of the snow, but the dogs had to plow through the deep drifts by sheer strength. Buck led the pack of sixty dogs around bend after bend of the creek. His splendid body leaped forward in the moonlight, but the rabbit still ran ahead.

Spitz was more experienced at this type of hunting, so he left the pack and cut across the narrow neck of land where the creek bent around. Soon, he was in the path of the on-rushing rabbit. Spitz leaped down from the bank, a white streak from above onto a white streak going by. The rabbit could not turn—the dog pack was behind it. It met its end in Spitz's teeth.

When Buck saw the rabbit snatched from him and the thrill of the chase ended by Spitz, he knew the time had come. He did not check his all-out run, but dove in on Spitz. Shoulder met shoulder, and the two went down in the powdery snow. Spitz got back on his feet almost as though he had not been overthrown. He slashed Buck across the shoulder and leaped clear. Then they circled one another, snapping and snarling. The other dogs made short work of the rabbit,

Spitz Captures the Rabbit.

then silently arranged themselves in a circle around Buck and Spitz.

Spitz had beaten all kinds of dogs in fights. He fought coldly and shrewdly. Buck rushed him again and again, but it was in vain. Every attack was defended easily, often with a parting slash that ripped Buck's shoulder. Buck then pretended to rush at Spitz's throat, but swerved to cut his shoulder. Spitz was too experienced for this tactic. He met Buck's rush with a slash that tore Buck's unguarded shoulder again. Then Spitz flashed back to circle around him.

The fight was growing one-sided. Spitz was untouched while Buck streamed blood. The silent, wolfish circle waited to finish off whichever dog went down. As Buck grew winded, Spitz took to rushing him. Buck staggered to get his footing, but fell over. The circle of dogs seemed ready to attack, but Buck recovered himself, almost in mid-air,

The Long-Awaited Fight!

and the waiting dogs sat down again.

Up to now, Buck had been fighting by instinct. But he could also fight with his brain now that he found himself in a desperate situation. He rushed Spitz again, as if trying the same throat-but-really-the-shoulder trick. At the last instant, he went in low, almost on the snow. His teeth broke Spitz's left hind leg. Spitz fought on three legs until Buck repeated the trick. With two broken legs, Spitz was doomed. Now Buck made a final rush, meeting Spitz shoulder to shoulder squarely. His teeth aimed for the snow-white throat and closed on it.

Buck sprang back. The circle of dogs leaped forward. Buck, the champion, watched without pity. This was the way of the North: kill or be killed.

Buck Breaks Spitz's Leg.

An Empty Harness

CHAPTER 14

Buck Makes Himself Lead-Dog

The next morning when François found Buck covered with wounds and Spitz missing, he knew instantly that the fight to the finish had taken place at last.

"That some dog, that Spitz!" he said. "Best lead-dog I ever see. Great fighter too. See wounds all over Buck, Perrault."

"Not as good a fighter as Buck," pointed out Perrault, "or *he* would be here, not Buck. Maybe for the best. Now we make good time. No more trouble because of Spitz."

François started to harness the dogs. He

took Sol-leks from his usual place and brought him to the front of the line. But Buck had placed himself there.

"What you think, Buck?" asked Francois with a laugh. "Just because you kill Spitz you can be leader? Go away! Back in line!"

Instead, Buck sprang at Sol-leks in a fury, driving him back to his original place. Then he stood again at the head. He would not budge until François dragged him away by the scruff of the neck.

Sol-leks was moved up again, but he did not like it and showed plainly that he was afraid of Buck. As soon as François turned to fasten the harness, Buck snarled at Sol-leks, who was eager to leave and did so in a hurry.

François was no longer amused. He picked up a club and waved it at Buck. Buck retreated slowly and allowed Sol-leks to be brought forward for the third time. François harnessed him as lead-dog. After all the dogs

Buck Wants to Be Lead-Dog.

except Buck were in the traces, François called him. Buck stayed where he was. When François tried to grab him, he retreated just out of reach. François threw down his club to show that no beating was intended. But it was not a whipping that Buck was concerned about. He had earned the lead position. He would not be content with less.

Perrault and François chased Buck for almost an hour. They threw clubs at him, but never connected. They swore at him and he snarled back. By not running out of the camp, Buck showed that he was ready at any moment to be harnessed—but only at the head of the team.

Perrault took another look at his watch and swore. They should have been on the trail over an hour ago. François grinned sheepishly and shrugged his shoulders. He unharnessed Sol-leks and returned him to his old place. Then he called Buck, and with a

Buck Refuses to Obey.

big smile, Buck came to him promptly. Buck had made himself lead-dog.

Buck took up his new duties with enthusiasm. Where judgment, quick thinking, and quick action were needed, Buck soon showed himself the superior of Spitz. One of the first things he did was to whip the team back into obedience. Dave and Sol-leks did not care who was in charge of the team. They did their work and wanted no interference. But the other dogs had developed bad habits through Buck's rebellion against Spitz.

Buck, however, showed them at once that the situation had changed. Pike was punished for not pulling with all his strength. Then Joe was beaten. And Billee too. All the dogs were whipped except Dave and Sol-leks.

In a few days, the old team spirit was back. The team pulled again like one dog. Their morale rose. François and Perrault were

A New Lead-Dog

happy and amazed at the speed that Buck got from the team.

At the Rink Rapids two native Huskies, Teek and Koona, were added. The speed with which Buck broke them in took François's breath away. He thought he had seen everything in lead-dogs, but Buck's ability to rule and his great intelligence and good judgment were new wonders to him.

The trail was in excellent condition with no new-fallen snow. Thus, on the trip back over the Thirty Mile River, they covered in one day what had taken them ten days before.

At Skagway they took count: for fourteen days they had averaged forty miles a day. Buck had led a record-breaking run!

A Record-Breaking Run!

A Tearful Good-Bye

CHAPTER 15

Visions of Primitive Times

One morning François and Perrault received official orders. They had been reassigned by the Canadian Government to an instruction center. There, they would train new messengers for life on the trail.

François called Buck to him. He threw his arms around him and wept. Then he and Perrault said good-bye to the other dogs. Buck never saw either of them again.

The team was transferred to ordinary mail carrying. Now they ran in company with a dozen other dog-teams known as the Salt

Water Mail. The sleds were loaded with mail to and from the gold seekers and their families back home. It was heavy work, and Buck did not like it. But he did it to the best of his ability and saw to it that the other dogs did also. Still, it was a monotonous life. They ran like machines, and one day was very like another. At the same time each morning, the cooks came out. Fires were built, and breakfast was eaten. Then, while some of the men broke camp, others harnessed the dogs. They were under way an hour or so before the first streaks of dawn. At night, camp was made. Some of the men set up the tents, while others cut firewood, gathered pine boughs for beds, and carried water or ice for the cooks.

Also the dogs were fed now. After the fish was eaten, the dogs liked to loaf around for an hour or so· with one another. They were over fifty in number, and many were fierce

The Salt Water Mail

fighters. Buck had three battles with th
fiercest dogs and won them all. As a result
when he bristled and showed his teeth, al
the dogs got out of his way.

Though Buck's dinner was very importan
to him and though he was proud of being the
master of all the dogs in camp, there wa
something else that he liked better. This wa
to lie near the fire with his hind leg
crouched under him and his fore legs
stretched out in front. His eyes blinked
dreamily at the flames. Sometimes he remembered Judge Miller's big house and the
swimming pool and stable. But more often he
thought of Morgan and the first fight when
he had been clubbed, or the death of Curly,
or the great fight with Spitz.

As he crouched before the flames, it seemed
that the fire was another one. . .one that he
or one of his ancestors had once crouched by.
And he had visions of a man seated beside

Remembering. . . .

him. . .a man who looked different from the men around him now. The man in his vision had short legs and long arms. His hair was long and matted. He was very frightened of the dark, and he peered into it constantly alert to the slightest sound.

Buck could see, too, that beyond the fire in the darkness were two round gleams of light. . .always two by two. He knew they were the eyes of great beasts of prey—the same beasts that the hairy man once feared.

In this way, Buck thought about things he had never known in his own life, only things his ancestors had known. It was the dancing flames that carried the strange messages from generation to generation, from a primitive cave to an ice-bound camp.

Visions of an Ancient World

A Soft Trail Means Heavier Pulling.

CHAPTER 16

Buck Is Sold Once More

When Buck and the team left Dawson for Skagway, it began to snow. This meant a soft trail, greater friction on the runners of the sleds, and heavier pulling for the dogs. They had already traveled eighteen hundred miles since the beginning of winter, and they began this trip with little strength. Gentle Billee whimpered regularly in his sleep at night.

Thirty days later, Buck and the other fifty dogs pulled into Skagway. They were in a terrible state. Buck's one hundred forty pounds had gone down to one hundred fifteen. Most of the dogs were limping, and some had suffered wrenched muscles. They were dead tired with no reserve strength to call upon. On the down grades they just about managed to keep out of the way of the sled as it flew behind them.

The drivers had expected a long stopover. But the mail had become an unending flood, and official orders awaited them. Fresh dogs were to be bought, and the used ones sold. The mail had to go through immediately. Buck and his team were put up for sale. They waited for three days before anyone gave them more than a second glance. Any experienced driver could tell that these dogs were worn out, and it would be a waste of feed money to buy them before they had regained their strength.

On the morning of the fourth day, two men from Virginia bought Buck's complete team and their harness very cheaply. One of the

Used, Worn-Out Dogs for Sale

men, Charles, was a middle-aged man with weak eyes that watered a great deal. His companion, Hal, was about twenty years old. He wore a belt with a hunting knife, a Colt revolver, and a large quantity of cartridges spaced around it. This belt advertised how important he believed himself to be, but it actually advertised how immature he was. The old-timers around Skagway hid a smile when they saw him and his huge belt approach.

Such were the two men who now owned Buck.

The Tenderfoot Hal

The Camp of Buck's New Owners

CHAPTER 17

The Tenderfeet

Charles and Hal drove their newly acquired team to their camp. Buck was amazed at its mess. The tent was half-stretched, the dishes unwashed, and everything was in disorder. There was also Mercedes. She was Charles' wife and Hal's sister. Even though she was as inexperienced in trail life as the men, she kept offering a stream of advice about loading, but offered no actual help in doing it. With a great deal of effort but no efficient method, the men rolled the tent into an awkward bundle. The tin dishes were packed away, still unwashed. Mercedes was very particular where her many bundles of clothes should ride, and she forced the men to reload them many times so they would always be handy for her. Finally everything was stowed.

Three men from the next tent had watched the loading with grins and winks at one another. One spoke up at last.

"It's not for me to tell you your business," he said, "but I wouldn't tote that tent along if I was you."

Mercedes gave him a look of dismay. "I have to have my tent! I couldn't manage without one. No, the tent goes with us."

"It's springtime," the man replied. "No more cold weather coming."

But Mercedes turned away from him and watched Charles lash up the huge load.

Another of the watchers said, "Seems a bit top-heavy, if you ask me."

Mercedes Directs the Loading.

Charles replied with an angry look. He picked up his whip and called loudly to the dogs, "Mush! Mush on there!"

Buck and the team tried to spring forward, but could not budge the load. They relaxed for a moment, then strained again against their breastbands. Nothing moved.

Hal snatched up his whip. "The lazy brutes! I'll show 'em!"

Mercedes stopped him with a cry, then tore the whip from his hand. "I won't have them whipped. You have to promise not to touch the dear things for the rest of the trip or I won't go. Now promise."

Her brother sneered. "A lot you know about dogs. You *have* to whip them to get any work out of them. That's the way it's done. You ask those men over there."

Mercedes appealed to the three neighbors with a pained expression. "Must he whip them? I can't stand to see it."

"I Won't Have Them Whipped."

The man who had first spoken answered her. "They're weak as water, if you want to know. Tuckered out. Only a good rest will put them right. I'm afraid you got stuck on this deal, whatever you paid."

At this open criticism of her menfolk's business abilities, Mercedes changed her mind. She gave her brother back his whip. "You do what you have to. We want to get started. We especially want to get away from here." She said this last with a sniff at the three watching men.

Hal's whip fell on the team. The dogs threw themselves against their breastbands and dug their feet into the packed snow, but the sled didn't move. Again the whip fell. And again. But the sled stayed as if it were anchored beneath the snow.

The oldest of the three men now came forward angrily. "I don't care a whoop what becomes of you or if you ever get on the trail.

A Neighbor's Advice Is Refused.

But for the dogs' sake, I just want to tell you to break out the sled and that will help them a lot. The runners are frozen fast. So throw your weight against the gee-pole, left and right. That will knock the runners loose."

Without a word of thanks, Hal and Charles broke out the sled. Now Buck and the team started forward at a creep under a rain of blows from the whip. Ahead, the path turned and sloped steeply into Skagway's main street. Perhaps an experienced driver might have been able to keep the top-heavy sled upright on the steep turn, but with Charles in charge, there was no chance. The sled went over, spilling half its load as a result of loose lashings.

The dogs never stopped. The now-light sled bounded on its side behind them. Buck was furious because of the cruel treatment and the unjust load, so he broke into a run. The team followed his lead, dashing through the

The Sled Goes Over!

main street of Skagway, scattering Mercedes' clothes bundles and the unwashed dishes everywhere.

Kind-hearted townspeople caught the dogs, gathered up the bundles, and gave advice. When the load was cut in half, they still shook their heads at the weight. So Charles and Hal bought six more dogs, but these dogs were all new to the North and didn't have the heart or the strength for trail life.

But the three tenderfoot Virginians were proud because they had never seen one sled with fourteen dogs except theirs. It never occurred to them that there must be a reason why they had never seen such a thing. It was simply that one sled could not carry enough food for fourteen dogs.

Thus the three Virginians set off ignorantly and arrogantly into the wilds with Buck as their lead-dog.

Six New Dogs for the Team

The Tenderfeet Never Learn.

CHAPTER 18

Suffering on the Trail

Charles, Hal, and Mercedes were full of energy and excitement. Their dogs were just the opposite. The team was still dead weary from the work with the mail sled.

As the days went by, Buck realized there was another problem—his owners did not know how to do anything to maintain a successful life on the trail. What was worse, they did not learn. It took them half the night to pitch their messy camp and half the morning to break it and get the sled loaded. On the trail they had to stop constantly to rearrange the load so it would ride correctly. Some days they did not make ten miles.

Hal had figured out the amount of dog food needed based on a certain number of days on the trail. It soon became apparent that they were far behind schedule and that the dog food would not last. Since none could be bought until the next town, there was only one solution—each dog got only half the ration he was accustomed to. It was well known that dogs imported to the North had to have much more food than the native Huskies. But Hal persisted in cutting down. This half ration led to the starvation of the six dogs bought in Skagway on the day they left. And though his teammates were dying, Buck continued to pull loyally.

His owners were doing even worse than the team. At first, Mercedes had wept over the dogs and had fed them on the sly. But soon her own problems took all her attention. She

Cutting the Food Ration in Half

and her husband and brother quarreled al
the time. Mostly it was over the work, each
accusing the other of not doing his share
From there, the quarrels would bring up old
family problems concerning people thousands
of miles away or even dead. They even ar-
gued over differences of opinion on art and
politics. While the fighting was going on, no
one worked. Precious hours needed to set up
or break camp were lost in the trading of
angry words.

Mercedes also found that the change in the
way she was being treated was too much to
bear. All her life she had been used to acting
like a helpless woman. It was the custom in
Virginia for women to be spoken to gently
and charmingly and to be taken care of by
men. Now the rude words and harsh treatment from her menfolk were a shock. She
struck back by insisting on riding in the
overloaded sled. Hal and Charles pleaded

Constant Quarrels!

with her. They rightly pointed out that her one hundred twenty pounds would be the last straw for the weak and starving team, but she won out.

After several days, the weak, starving animals finally fell down. The sled stood still. After begging and ordering Mercedes off the sled with no result, the men simply lifted her off. She let her legs go limp, like a spoiled child, and sat down on the trail. The men continued on their way, but she did not move. After they had traveled three miles, they gave in and returned for her. They lifted her back on the sled and inched along.

This was also the day that the dog food finally gave out.

Buck staggered along in a nightmare. He pulled when he could. When he could no longer pull, he fell down until blows from a club or whip drove him to his feet. All the stiffness and gloss had gone out of his beautiful

A Temper Tantrum!

furry coat. The hair hung down, limp and draggled, or matted with dried blood where Hal's club had bruised him. Each rib was outlined clearly through his loose hide. The team looked like skeletons creeping along. One by one they fell and could not rise. Hal was forced to kill three of them to end their suffering.

Only Buck and four other dogs remained as they pulled up beside a one-man camp near the White River. It was spring, and the trees and ice, alike, were thawing and bending and snapping. When the team stopped, the dogs fell where they were as if dead. Mercedes was crying as usual. The two men were staggering from weariness and disillusionment.

The owner of the camp was sitting on a log, whittling the last touches on an axe handle he had made from a stick of birch. Buck lifted his exhausted head and saw John Thornton for the first time.

Starved and Worked to Death

John Thornton Offers Advice.

CHAPTER 19

Buck Is Rescued

Thornton sized up the three people for the arrogant tenderfeet they were. When Hal had asked about the condition of the ice, Thornton had simply replied, "Rotten!" But Thornton knew they would ignore this advice. And they did.

Hal gave a skeptical smile. "That's what we heard two days ago, that the bottom was dropping out of the trail. Some men told us we wouldn't be able to make White River, and here we are," he boasted triumphantly.

"Those men were right," said Thornton.

"The bottom's likely to drop out at any moment. Only a lucky fool could have made it here. Me, I wouldn't go out on that ice on the river for all the gold in Alaska. My advice is stay put."

"Don't you worry about us," said Hal with a slight sneer. "Some of us are a little braver than others. It wouldn't surprise me a bit if we didn't pull into Dawson before you know it, rotten ice or no rotten ice." He uncoiled his whip and shouted, "Get up there, Buck! Hi! Mush on!"

But the team did not get up. Hal bore down with his whip. John Thornton's lips tightened, but he did not speak. Sol-leks was the first to crawl to his feet. Joe made two painful tries and fell over each time. On the third try, he managed to stand. Buck made no effort. He lay quietly where he had fallen. The lash bit into him again and again, but he neither whined nor struggled. Several times

Too Exhausted to Get Up

Thornton started to speak, then stopped himself.

This was the first time that Buck had failed, and it drove Hal into a rage to have it happen before this trail-wise stranger. He threw down the whip and used a club on Buck. Like the other dogs, Buck could just about have managed to get up. There was one difference—Buck had made up his mind *not* to get up. He had a vague feeling of doom. All day he had noticed thin, rotten ice under his feet. Now he strongly sensed disaster if he went back on the icy river. So he refused to stir.

So greatly had Buck suffered and so near death was he that the blows from Hal's club did not hurt much. Buck felt strangely numb though he was aware that the club continued to fall heavily. His life was flickering out. His eyes were closing.

Suddenly, without warning, there was a

Buck Is Near Death.

furious cry, more like an animal's than a man's. It was John Thornton. He sprang at Hal and knocked him down with one blow.

Standing over Buck, Thornton spoke to Hal in a voice thick with rage. "If you strike that dog again, I'll kill you!"

"It's my dog," said Hal, rising and wiping the blood from his nose. "Get out of my way or I'll fix you! I'm going to Dawson and I'm going now!"

Thornton continued to stand his ground between Hal and Buck. Mercedes screamed as Hal drew out his hunting knife. But Thornton, with an easy flick of his wrist, rapped Hal's knuckles with the axe-handle. Hal dropped the knife. As he dove after it, Thornton rapped his hand again even harder. Then he picked up the knife himself and cut Buck's traces.

Hal had no fight left in him after the strains of travel with Charles and Mercedes

Thornton Knocks Hal Down.

and their ill fortune. He decided that Buck would soon be dead anyway, so he gave in to Thornton. He picked up his knife and whip and club, then forced the four remaining dogs back on the icy river.

Buck heard them leave, and he raised his head to see. Pike was leading, with Sol-leks at the wheel. In between were Joe and Teek. They were limping and staggering. Mercedes was riding, Hal was guiding at the gee-pole, and Charles was stumbling along behind the sled.

As Buck watched, Thornton knelt beside him. His rough, kindly hands searched for broken bones. By the time he had decided that Buck's problems were countless bruises and a terrible state of starvation, the sled was already on the frozen river.

Buck and Thornton watched it crawling along over the ice. Suddenly they saw its back end drop down, as if into a rut. The

The Sled Goes On Without Buck.

gee-pole, with Hal clinging to it, jerked into the air. Mercedes' scream reached their ears. They saw Charles turn and take one step to run back to shore. Then a whole section of ice gave way. Dogs and people disappeared. Only a huge watery hole remained. Buck finally understood what people meant when they said that the bottom had dropped out of the trail!

John Thornton and Buck looked at each other. "You poor devil," said Thornton.

Buck licked his hand.

The Bottom Drops Out of the Trail.

Buck Regains His Strength.

CHAPTER 20

Buck and John Thornton

John Thornton was alone in camp with only two dogs because he was recovering from frozen feet. He was still limping slightly when Buck came into his life. Together, the two invalids sat on the river bank through the warm spring days, listening to the birds and watching the sparkling water. Thornton was expecting his partners to arrive from Dawson soon.

After three thousand miles of travel, Buck was able to rest at last. As his wounds healed, he regained his lost weight and glossy coat. Skeet, a little Irish setter, had taken the responsibility for Buck on his arrival. She had the doctor trait which some dogs possess. She washed and cleansed Buck's wounds like a mother cat washing her kitten. At first, Buck would have resisted these advances if he had had the strength. Later, he looked forward to the morning washing.

Nig was Thornton's other dog—a big, black fellow, half-bloodhound and half-deerhound. Both dogs' friendliness amazed Buck. Neither was jealous of Thornton's attention to him, so perhaps the man's kindness had brushed off onto his animals. He saw to them as if they were his children. He romped and played ridiculous games with them. Soon Buck found himself adoring this man.

Judge Miller had been a dignified old man, not given to romping with Buck. Buck had liked him and had enjoyed their stately friendship, but he had never experienced the

Skeet and Nig Befriend Buck.

burning passion he now felt for Thornton. It seemed as if all of Buck's life he had been storing up loyalty and adoration for such a master. Thornton had a way of taking Buck's head roughly between his large hands and resting his own head on Buck's. Then he would shake Buck's head back and forth, saying, "You old, ugly monster" and "You wicked thieving villain of a dog," which was all love-talk to the two of them. This rough embrace was Buck's greatest delight. Often it seemed as if his heart would burst with joy as it went on.

When Hans and Pete, Thornton's partners, arrived, Buck refused to notice them. After he learned that they were close to Thornton he tolerated them. The men understood Buck's attitude and did not try to force a friendship on him. Nig and Skeet liked all three men, pushing their heads under a hand in order to be petted. Thornton, especially,

Love-Talk Delights Buck.

would always respond to this demand. Bu
Buck would not ask for affection. He woul
only sit near Thornton and watch every ex
pression on his face. Every now and the
Buck's gaze was so intense that it cause
Thornton to look into Buck's adoring eyes
The two would hold that look for a moment
each one loving the other greatly.

Yet even as Buck sat happily by John
Thornton's fire, he saw visions of his wild an
cestors in the flames. And he heard the
call—the call of the wild. At that moment, a
hunger stirred in him—a hunger for the time
when all dogs were fierce and free, like
wolves.

Buck Hears the Call of the Wild.

"Black" Burton Picks a Fight.

CHAPTER 21

Buck Becomes Famous

That winter, John Thornton and his partners, Pete and Hans, traveled to Dawson because their money was getting low. Since Buck followed Thornton everywhere, he was lying nearby while the three men were having a drink at a bar.

"Black" Burton, an evil-tempered, malicious man, was also drinking there and had been for some time. He was a bully and never hesitated using his strong fists instead of words. Now he was picking a fight with a tenderfoot. The tenderfoot tried to apologize, but Burton was intent on a fight. He gave the man a rough push.

At this, John Thornton stepped in. His strong sense of fairness would not let him watch the innocent tenderfoot suffer. Thornton said a few quiet words, but suddenly Burton swore and struck out, straight from the shoulder. The blow sent Thornton spinning. He saved himself from falling by grabbing the rail of the bar.

The men around them heard a sound that was neither a bark nor a yelp. One man described it as a roar. They saw Buck's body rise up in the air and leap for Burton's throat. The man saved his life by instinctively throwing out his arm. But Buck's weight threw him to the floor. Buck had bitten his arm and was now going for his throat again. Burton tried to protect himself, but Buck tore at his flesh.

As Burton's blood started to flow, the

Buck Defends His Master.

onlookers woke from their amazement and drove Buck off. A doctor hurried forward, while Buck prowled around the crowd, growling furiously and trying to rush back at Burton. The crowd held a trial at once to decide on Buck's fate. Attacking a man was the most serious crime a dog could commit.

Their decision was unanimous—Buck had been provoked to an unusual degree and was justified in his action. From that moment on, Buck's name became famous in the North.

Throughout Alaska, a man's favorite dog was often the topic of conversation. Now, John Thornton was forced to defend Buck against much bragging. Because of Buck's reputation for heroism after his attack on Burton, other men used him as an example for their own dogs to follow and better.

During one such conversation, a man started the competition by claiming his dog could start a sled loaded with five hundred

Buck Is On Trial.

pounds and walk off with it. Another said that his dog could do six hundred pounds. A third jumped in with seven hundred. Then they looked at Thornton to hear what he would say.

When Thornton saw their challenging expressions, he rashly said, "That's nothing. Buck can start a *thousand* pounds!"

His listeners stared at him in disbelief. "What?" exclaimed one. "And break out the sled? And walk with it for a hundred yards?" The man was Mathewson, a rich prospector whose dog could do seven hundred pounds.

Thornton did not hesitate now that he had said it, even though "breaking out" a sled meant starting it while it was still frozen to the ground. Usually it was the driver who threw his weight from side to side to rock the sled loose. But could a dog do it by himself?

"Buck can break out a thousand pounds and walk one hundred yards with it,"

"Buck Can Start a *Thousand* Pounds!"

Thornton stated calmly.

"Well," said Mathewson slowly, "I've got a thousand dollars that says he can't. And here it is." With that, he slammed a bag full of gold dust on the table.

By now all other conversation in the room had stopped, and everyone was intent on Thornton's group. Thornton started to flush. His bluff was being called. His tongue had tricked him because he had no idea how much weight Buck could pull, much less break out. But a thousand pounds was half a ton! Besides, Thornton and his partners had only two hundred dollars among the three of them.

Mathewson saw his discomfort and gave a slight smile. "I've got a load of flour outside," he said. "Twenty sacks, each weighing fifty pounds. I suggest we go on out there and see what this wonder dog of yours can do with that thousand pounds."

A Bet Is Made.

Thornton didn't know what to say. Then he saw old Jim O'Brien standing with the others, waiting to hear his reply. Jim was Thornton's good friend, but he was also rich. Thornton leaned over to him and asked, "Jim, will you lend me a thousand dollars?"

"Sure I will," answered O'Brien, pulling a sack of gold dust from his back pocket and handing it to Thornton. "But I'm afraid you're going to get beat."

With the bet in, the crowd began to cheer, then followed Thornton and Mathewson outside. When Thornton looked at the loaded sled with its team of ten dogs needed to pull such a weight, his heart sank. The runners of the sled were firmly imbedded in the frozen grip of the snow.

As the crowd continued to make side bets, the odds against Buck rose from even money to three to one. *One dog move half a ton from a frozen standstill?* Impossible!

Buck's Test—*A Half-Ton Load!*

When Mathewson saw that the crowd agreed with his judgment and were not betting on Buck, he turned to Thornton again. "I'll up my bet another thousand. What do you say?"

After a quick conference with Hans and Pete, Thornton bet their two hundred dollars at three-to-one odds. Thus Mathewson was wagering another six hundred dollars.

The ten dogs were unhitched, and Buck, in his own harness, was put before the loaded sled. Murmurs of admiration arose at his appearance. Here was one hundred fifty pounds of iron encased in glossy fur.

One man was so entranced at the sight of such a magnificent animal that he offered John Thornton eight hundred dollars for Buck, without caring how the contest came out.

Thornton didn't even bother to answer. He waved the man back and knelt at Buck's

Mathewson Increases His Bet.

side. Taking the dog's head in his hands and resting his cheek against Buck's, he whispered, "Pull, Buck. If you love me, pull with everything that's in you."

As his answer, Buck seized Thornton's mittened hand between his jaws and held it there for a moment. His sharp teeth were as gentle as silk. It was a gesture that showed Buck's love and determination.

Thornton stepped well back. "Now, Buck," he said as Buck watched him. "Now, gee!" Thornton's voice rang out over the silent crowd.

Buck swung to the right with a jerk. The plunge of his weight caused the load to quiver. From under the runners arose a crisp crackling sound.

"Haw!" commanded Thornton.

Buck made the same maneuver to the left. The crackling turned into a snapping. The sled pivoted, and the runners slipped. The

Buck "Breaks Out" the Sled.

sled was broken out! The watching men hardly breathed.

The final command came like a pistol shot. "Now, MUSH!"

Buck threw himself forward, tightening the traces with a jarring lunge. His entire body was concentrated in the tremendous effort. His great chest was low to the ground and his head was forward and down. His feet flew madly, the claws scarring the hard-packed snow into grooves.

The sled swayed and trembled. Then it half-started forward. The crowd groaned as one of Buck's feet slipped. Then the sled went ahead in a rapid succession of tiny jerks ...half an inch...an inch...two inches.... The jerks merged into a glide as Buck gained momentum. The sled was moving steadily.

The crowd gasped. Thornton ran behind, encouraging Buck. As Buck neared the one-hundred-yard mark, a pile of firewood, the

Can Buck Pull the Load 100 Yards?

crowd started to cheer. When Buck passed the firewood, the cheers grew to a roar. Everyone was shouting and throwing hats and mittens into the air, even the loser Mathewson. Men were shaking hands all around, it did not matter with whom. Over and over they explained to each other what a wonderful thing they had just seen, just as if the listeners had not been there too. Jim O'Brien bought everyone a drink, and they toasted Buck with it.

Thornton was on his knees beside Buck, head against head. He was almost choking as he repeated the familiar, loving words, "You big old villain, Buck. You wicked monster."

The man who had wanted to buy Buck before the contest interrupted Thornton's conversation with Buck. "What a dog! I'll give you twelve hundred dollars for him!"

Thornton rose to his feet. "No, sir. I would sooner sell myself into slavery than part with

Victory!

Buck. Don't ask me again."

And that statement, too, became part of the legend in Alaska when men who had been there told newcomers about the day in Dawson when John Thornton's dog, Buck, broke out a half ton and walked one hundred yards with it. Buck had become famous!

Thornton Refuses to Sell Buck.

New Equipment for the Gold Seekers

CHAPTER 22

Buck Finds a Brother

Buck had earned sixteen hundred dollars in five minutes. Thornton, Pete, and Hans could hardly believe their changed luck, for now they had the money to outfit themselves as gold seekers.

They set off with Buck and six other dogs on the first leg of their journey, seventy miles up the Yukon. They traveled slowly in Indian fashion, hunting their food as they went. The sled carried mainly tools and ammunition. To Buck, the trip was an endless delight, just fishing, hunting, and wandering in strange

places. Sometimes the men and dogs went
hungry; sometimes they feasted. It all de-
pended on the fortunes of the hunt.

When summer arrived, the men built rafts
and pushed out across blue mountain lakes.
They picked strawberries and enjoyed the
flowers blooming in the shadow of glaciers.

Fall, winter, and another spring passed before they came to a broad valley. There, they
found a stream that left a deposit of gold in
the bottom of the washing-pans.

They didn't have to go any farther. They
set up camp and got to work. Every day that
they panned the little stream, they came up
with thousands of dollars in nuggets and
clean gold dust. Soon moose-hide bags, each
holding fifty pounds of gold, were stacked
like firewood, making a pile even taller than
Buck.

Except for an occasional hunting expedition
for food with Thornton, Buck had nothing to

Thousands of Dollars in Gold Nuggets!

do. More and more of his time was taken up by gazing into the fire. He saw visions of the hairy man in the flames. Sometimes the man was alert, sometimes he was fearful. Buck often saw him sleeping in a tree while Buck's ancestor—or was it Buck himself?—kept a watch below. And then Buck would hear the strange call—the wolf's mournful song that seemed to be calling him. He would dash from camp and roam for hours looking for the source of that song. . .looking unsuccessfully.

One night Buck sprang out of camp after a deep sleep in which he heard the long, drawn-out howl. He ran for miles in the moonlight, then stopped suddenly. He proceeded with caution toward an open place among the trees. Looking out from the bushes, Buck saw a lean timber wolf, erect on his haunches, with his nose pointed to the sky. The wolf sensed Buck's presence.

When Buck came out into the open, half-

Buck Sees a Timber Wolf.

crouching, his tail was straight and stiff. He gave an appearance of friendliness and, at the same time, a threat.

The wolf fled at the sight of him. Buck pursued. Snarling, the wolf whirled about, but Buck did not attack. He only circled and made friendly advances. But the wolf was suspicious. At the first chance he darted away, with Buck after him. Buck weighed three times as much as the wolf. And the wolf's head barely came to Buck's shoulder, so he could not understand why Buck held off attacking. At last, Buck's persistence was rewarded. The wolf halted.

He allowed Buck to advance, and they sniffed noses. Then they became friendly and played. After a time, the wolf started off in a manner that plainly showed he had a goal in mind. He also made it clear that Buck was to come too. The two loped along easily, mile after mile through the woods. Buck felt

A New Friend

wildly happy because he knew he was at last answering the call—the call of the wild. He was running side by side with his brother toward the place from where the call surely came. He felt he had done this thing before. . .somewhere, sometime.

They stopped by a stream to drink. And there, Buck remembered John Thornton. He sat down. The wolf started on again, but Buck did not follow. Confused, the wolf returned for him again and again, sniffing his nose and encouraging him to go on.

But Buck turned and started running the opposite way. For almost an hour the wolf ran with him, back the way they had come, all the time whining softly. Then he sat down, pointed his nose upward, and howled. It was a mournful sound. As Buck ran steadily homeward, he heard the cry grow fainter and fainter until, at last, it was lost in the distance, lost in the trees.

Buck Returns Home.

Buck Gets Restless.

CHAPTER 23

Attack of the Yeehats

For two days and two nights Buck never left camp and never let John Thornton out of his sight. But then his restlessness came back. The urge to be part of life in the forest became greater than ever before, and Buck responded. He began to sleep in the woods at night. Often he would stay away for days at a time. He killed his meat as he traveled and always, he watched for signs of his wild brother.

In the forest Buck was a different animal from the romping one in camp. He became a creature of the wild, stealing along softly, cat-footed. He was like a passing shadow, moving so quickly that he could scoop a fish from an open pool. He even stalked an old moose, cut him off from his herd, and brought him down. The hunt took days, but Buck was tireless and persistent. Then he was ready to go home again.

Three miles from camp he came upon a scent that disturbed him. He proceeded faster, but more cautiously. Then his nose was jerked from the trail to the bushes. There he found Nig, dead, with an arrow embedded in his body.

From the camp came a sing-song chant of many voices. Buck crept forward and saw Hans lying next to the bags of gold. His body was studded with arrows. Nearby, the Yeehats, an Indian tribe, were dancing a victory dance around the fire. Rage came over Buck like rolls of thunder. He hurled himself

A Terrible Discovery!

out of the bushes onto the dancers.

The Yeehats heard a fearful roar. Like a hurricane, Buck struck down their chief, ripping his throat wide open. With the next bound he had felled another Indian. Before the Yeehats realized what was happening, Buck had killed five of them. They ran for their weapons and let loose a fury of arrows.

But Buck's movements were so rapid and the Yeehats were grouped so closely together that the arrows pierced the Indians themselves instead of the dog. As Buck continued his rampage without slowing down or missing his targets, the Yeehats panicked. Shouting that the Evil Spirit was among them, the Indians scattered through the woods. Buck chased after them, pulling them down a man at a time. Finally tiring of the pursuit, he ran back to camp.

It was not until a week later that the Indians who survived were able to find one

Buck, the Avenger!

another in a lower valley. There, they counted their enormous losses.

In camp, Buck found Pete dead in his blankets. But where was his beloved master? Buck picked up John Thornton's scent and followed it to a stream. On the bank there was evidence of a fierce fight. Thornton's trail led into the water, but it did not lead away. Buck understood what death was, and he knew that John Thornton was dead.

All day Buck sat by the stream or roamed restlessly around camp. There was a great emptiness in him, one that ached like hunger. But no food could fill it. At times he stopped in his aimless prowling and looked at the bodies of the Yeehats. For a moment he would forget the pain of Thornton's death because a certain pride filled him. He had killed Man, and Man was game forbidden to beasts.

Buck Mourns John Thornton.

The Wolf Pack

CHAPTER 24

Buck Answers the Call of the Wild

Night came on with a full moon. Buck was mourning and brooding by the stream that held John Thornton's body. Suddenly he stood up, listening and scenting. From far away drifted a faint, sharp yelp, followed by a chorus of similar sharp yelps. As the moments passed, the yelps grew closer and louder. Buck recognized them as the sounds he had heard in that other world—the world which he half-saw, half-dreamed in front of the fire. It was the call—the call of the wild, and it was more wonderful and more compel-

ling than ever before. And now, as never be
fore, Buck was ready to answer it. John
Thornton was dead. Buck's last tie with Man
was broken.

The wolf pack had crossed over rivers and
timberland into Buck's valley. Now, with the
moonlight streaming down on them, they
poured in a silvery flood into a clearing. In
the center of the clearing stood Buck, motion
less, waiting for them.

The pack was awed for a moment at this
immense, still creature. Then the boldest
leaped straight at him. Like a flash, Buck
struck. The wolf's neck was broken by a
single charge. Buck waited again, motionless as
before. Three more wolves leaped for him,
and one after the other they retreated with
slashed throats or shoulders.

Now the whole pack, almost as one, flung
itself at Buck. But he turned on his hind legs,
from side to side, snapping and gashing. H

Surrounded by Enemies

was everywhere at once, whirling so fast tha
he presented an unbroken front of defense
Not a wolf could touch him.

To prevent the pack from getting behin
him, Buck was forced back, bit by bit. H
finally stood in a dry creek bed, backed agains
a deep bank the men had made in their min
ing. Here he stood at bay. With three side
protected, he faced the wolves and took or
each enraged animal.

After half an hour, Buck was still in com
mand. The pack had drawn back, laying o
standing in a ring around him, nursing their
wounds.

Then one wolf, long and lean and gray
advanced cautiously, in a friendly manner
Buck's eyes lit up as he recognized his wild
brother with whom he had run side by side
for hours. The wolf whined softly, and so did
Buck. They touched noses.

After him came an old wolf, gaunt and

An Old Friend Approaches Buck.

scarred from fighting. He put his face forward. After a moment's hesitation, Buck touched noses with him also. At this, the old wolf sat down, pointed his nose at the moon and broke out into the long wolf howl. The other wolves did the same. Buck, watching intently, felt his fur bristle. But this bristling was not from anger, but from the strangeness and mournfulness of the cry. He no longer held off, but sat down too and howled at the moon.

This over, Buck came out of his protected place. The pack crowded around him, sniffing in a half-friendly, half-savage manner. Then the leaders yelped and sprang away into the woods. The pack fell in behind, yelping in chorus. And Buck ran with them, side by side with his wild brother, yelping as he ran.

Buck Runs with His Wild Brother.

Robbing the Yeehats' Trap

CHAPTER 25

The Ghost Dog

It was not many years before the Yeehats noticed a change in the breed of timber wolves. Some were seen with splashes of brown on their head and muzzle. Others had strip of white running down the center of their chest.

But even more remarkable than this, the Yeehats also tell of a Ghost Dog that runs at the head of a pack. They fear his great strength, but more than that, they fear his cunning. No matter how they try to protect themselves, the Ghost Dog robs their traps,

237

steals from their camps, and kills their dogs. And from time to time, their hunters are found with throats slashed open and with wolf prints about them in the snow—prints larger than any wolf's ever seen.

The Yeehats also fear a certain valley where, legend has it, an Evil Spirit lives. They never hunt there, and women of the tribe grow sad when the valley is mentioned. There is, however, one visitor to the valley who goes there every summer. He looks like a wolf and yet not like a wolf. He sits brooding and sad for a long while by a stream. Then he howls once, a long and mournful howl, and leaves.

When the long winter nights come on, the Ghost Dog can be seen running at the head of a wolf pack through the pale moonlight. From time to time he raises his great head and with the pack, he sounds the call of the wild.

The Ghost Dog Sounds the Call of the Wild.

ILLUSTRATED CLASSIC EDITIONS